# THE ALIEN'S MISSION

GRACE KENSINGTON

ALIEN WARRIOR MATES II - BOOK 1

**1**

---

The Denynso warriors were lined up along the center of the compound facing the meeting hall, creating a powerful wall of intensity and strength. Each wore a black band around his arm, bold white stitches creating a "J" in the center. They were silent, stoic as they stared at the front steps of the hall where Creia, the king of their people, had appeared through the massive wooden doors.

Creia wore long black robes that stood in stark contrast to the blue of his usual clothing. The white of his hair intensified the darkness of the black ribbons woven through it that reflected the woven pattern through the hair of each of the warriors that faced him. There were several moments of dark, tense silence that hung over the compound and then the doors behind the king opened slowly.

Though they remained silent, the warriors stiffened. They all knew what was coming, and none of them felt prepared to handle it. It had only been twenty-four hours since the battle and they were all still trying to cope with the effects of the horror that they had seen. To overcome it, however, they knew they had to honor what was lost so that they could internalize their pain and anger, and move forward with even greater determination. The Klimnu were gone, but that didn't mean that they were always going to be safe, or that they would forget what they had to go through in order to get rid of those creatures.

Bannack fought the urge to shift in his position in the line of warriors. On either side of him were Pyra and Gyyx, both staring unblinking at the doors as they opened. The anger that built inside him was unlike anything he had ever experienced. Even as a member of a species of warriors known for being aggressive, intense, and powerful, he was volatile and unpredictable. Younger than most of the other warriors, Bannack had not seen as many battles as the others, but this had been something that he could never have fathomed. What he had seen had scarred him in a place deeper than he understood, and as he stood there watching the first of the women appear at the door.

Tall and strong, the Denynso women seemed far more powerful than the females of the other species they had encountered, but in that moment each stood at the door with tears streaming down their faces. None made a sound despite the tears. They stayed strong, keeping their eyes focused ahead of them with the same concentration and intensity as the warriors. After standing in the doorway for a few moments, the women stepped forward and the black cloth they held between them came into view.

The cloth held a folded tunic and a small dagger in the center, and the women held it as if they could feel the strange lack of weight that usually accompanied the funeral cloth when they made their processional down the steps of the meeting hall and toward the wide lake at the back of the compound. Suddenly the king's voice broke through the intense silence that felt like it was suffocating the warriors.

"Today we honor one of our own who has fallen. Jem fought valiantly in our battles against the Klimnu and in his last moments he made the most courageous decision that he could. With his last breaths he chose to sacrifice himself for the good and the future of our kind. With his death he took with him the last of our most hated of enemies, securing for us a future that is free from their torment and primed for the joy that will come. We will never forget what he did for us and though we cannot properly honor his body, we honor his memory and the bit of him that will continue with us forever."

As Creia fell silent again, the women continued forward from their place to the meeting hall and down the imposing stone stairs. Those stairs always represented the strength and stability of the species and the security of the compound, but now they seemed to emphasize the pain that radiated through the row of warriors and the women who carried the empty shroud down them. As they descended, the women didn't make eye contact with any of the warriors. This was their way. The women carried the dead, a final symbol of nurturing and care, while the warriors stood vigil as a sign of continuous protection and respect.

Bannack could see the tears sparkling on the women's cheeks and felt discomfort in his stomach. The women of their kind were not known to be emotional and only one other time in his life had he seen one of them shed a single tear. Now they were all crying, though restraining any noise, and he knew that it was not just for Jem, the warrior who had sacrificed himself in the final battle of a lengthy war against the evil Klimnu species. They were crying for everything that their kind had gone through in their years of battle against the slimy creatures who had been so determined to capture and kill their beloved king Creia and take over the compound, and the entirety of the planet of Uoria. They were crying for everything that those creatures had put the Denynyso through, and everything that they had done to the human women who had come to the planet and become a part of the clan. It was perhaps these women, the smaller, more delicate human women, who had suffered the worst at the hands of the Klimnu in recent times, and it was them that had given the Denynso warriors what they needed to finally defeat them.

The women carried the black cloth with Jem's tunic and dagger, the personal items they had taken from his home to represent him in the absence of his actual body, down the steps and through the center of the compound, passing through the line of warriors that separated silently as they approached. Bannack felt the anger become even more intense as his eyes fell on the empty tunic. This wasn't fair. This wasn't what one of the strongest, bravest, and most self-less men to have ever been in their clan deserved for his final memorial. He deserved to have his body honored in the way of the men that came before him, and to be offered the same respect that any of the other warriors would expect if they were the ones who had given their lives to finally bring the conflict with the Klimnu to an end. It was if the slimy, vile creatures had gotten their last bit of vengeance even though they were eradicated in the battle. By giving himself, wholly and completely, Jem had saved the Denynso, but had also given the Klimnu a grasp on the history of the clan that they would never be able to shake free. Whenever someone thought or spoke of Jem, they would be forced to think and speak of the Klimnu as well.

Bannack kept his eyes forward as the women passed through the line of warriors, trying to tear his mind away from the thoughts of that final battle that had been tormenting him for the last day. They flashed in front of his eyes as if they were still happening, filling his mind with reverberations of the sounds, the smells, and the gut-wrenching pain. He remembered the exact moment that the battle had ended. It was unlike any other battle that they had ever experienced with the Klimnu. Those battles had ended with the Klimnu retreating, running away from the vastly more powerful Denynso so that they could go back to planning their next attack. This battle, however, had ended when the final three Klimnu approached Jem on a branch in the mysterious mirrored world that existed just beneath the compound.

Though Ty, a young Denynso who had just learned to utilize a hidden gift that he had inherited from his father and had never used before to step out of his usual role and become a warrior, had attempted to save him, Jem knew what was better for the rest of the warriors, the compound, and all of Uoria. He had fought the power that would have lifted him out of the battle and saved his life. Instead, he grabbed onto the final three Klimnu and threw himself off of the branch, disappearing into the reflected sky and taking the creatures with him. The Denynso didn't know where he went or what had happened to him, but they knew that he would not return.

The ending of the battle had been so sudden, so intense and final, but Bannack still felt the aggression and anger that fueled them through the fighting. Entering that mirror world had been like nothing Bannack had ever experienced. In that world he felt more powerful, more intense, and more aggressive than he ever had in any other battle. There was something brewing inside him that he couldn't fight and he felt like he was on the brink of going insane.

## 2

B annack took his place near the edge of the lake and mimicked the position of the other warriors, reaching over his shoulder for one of the arrows tucked in the quiver on his back. His opposite hand held a bow painstakingly handcrafted from one of the trees in the forest that they had only the day before discovered was covering the mysterious and dangerous underground lair that the Klimnu had been using to infiltrate the compound with the help of a human flight attendant who sympathized with the Klimnu's hatred for the Denynso. This was a treasured weapon, but one almost never used for actual combat. Instead, it was an item that every Denynso warrior made for himself in his early life and kept as a reminder of their heritage and the ancestors. Occasionally the bows made an appearance during a battle or were used to hunt some of the species that would come to the land near the compound once a year. Most often, though, they were kept displayed within the warriors' homes and taken down only when it was time to pay homage to the dead.

The women carried the cloth to the edge of the purple

water, its color darker and more saturated than the smaller pond near the cliffs on the other edge of the compound, and lowered themselves to their knees. They moved in concert, never turning their eyes away from the intense focus directly in front of them, but moving at the same moments and in the exact same way as all of the others. The first two women lowered their corners of the cloth into the water and the women behind them handed their sections forward, passing the edges of the black shroud through all of their hands so that the first two could guide it down into the lake.

As the water took hold of the cloth and it started to drift forward, the warriors drew their arrows and lifted their bows. When the cloth made it nearly to the center of the lake, Creia walked down the row of warriors, lighting the ends of the arrows with the torch he held. The warriors lifted their flaming arrows at the same moment, pointing them sharply toward the expanse of dark blue above them, and let them fly.

The arrows hit the cloth just as it reached the center of the lake and a massive whirlpool began to churn beneath it. This majestic phenomenon was why the earliest members of the Denynso tribe had chosen this lake as the place where they would put their cherished warrior to final rest. The whirlpool began when something touched the center of the lake and would churn as it did now, pushing upward into a funnel of water that lifted the flame-engulfed cloth, tunic, and dagger toward the sky. After several seconds, the column of water lowered and the flames, along with the memorial to Jem, disappeared into the depths. They didn't know what happened to the honored men that ended up in the water, but they believed that by giving them into the water that surged under the ground and gave life to the plants that thrived on Uoria, they were giving their beloved warriors continued life.

Bannack could only hope that it was true now. Jem's death was a confounding and infuriating mystery that none of the warriors, and not even Creia or his wife, the queen of the Denynso Theia, could explain. What lurked beneath the compound was a place that seemed to directly reflect the land above it, as if a mirror had been placed just at the ground line so that what looked like branches of massive trees were actually the roots above, what looked like roots were actually branches, and what looked like water covering the floor of the massive cavern was actually a reflection of the sky. This is where Jem fell. He jumped down into this reflection of the sky, giving himself over to it without knowing what would happen, and none knew where he ended up.

Bannack hoped that even though they could not properly inter his body in the lake, that Jem's spirit would continue on through all of them and give them the strength and courage that he possessed, because even though they had eliminated the last of the Klimnu, Bannack did not believe that it would be the end of the threats to the Denynso. There would be more. There would be more battles to fight and more wars to win, and each warrior was going to need every bit of intensity and power that he could have if he was going to be able to help his kind continue to thrive and dominate their part of Uoria.

EVERYONE STAYED in their places by the lake for several minutes after the funnel of water had completely disappeared back into the lake and the surface had become calm again. The women remained kneeling in the sand, the warriors maintained their wall of defiance, and the king and queen stood stoic and calm on the opposite side of the women. Behind them, a few yards back from this ritual that they had not seen and would not understand, stood the human women who had made their home on Uoria. These women, the mates of some of the warriors, as well as the healer and the baker, were astonishing to him.

He, like many of the other Denynso, had thought of human women as weak, flimsy little creatures prone to extreme emotions and unlikely to make much of a contribution to anything. When Creia announced that he wanted to foster greater understanding, connection, and cooperation with the humans of Earth, and that humans would be coming to the planet in order to not only research them, but to help them understand humankind, many of the warriors had been skeptical, even angry. Many of the earliest visitors, primarily scientists, had only been after a sample of their blood. It was well known that the blood of the Denynso warriors was incredibly special, and that it held the key to not only their powers and abilities, but to many amazing uses. Their desire to take samples of their blood had only increased the distrust among many of the warriors.

Eden had changed that. She was the first of the human women to show up on the planet and to earn their trust. The mate of Pyra, the most powerful and revered warrior among them, Eden was not standing with the other human women. Instead, she was kneeling in the sand at the edge of the lake with the Denynso women. This was because she had faced a brutal death at the claws of a Klimnu who had made his way into the compound by guising himself as Pyra. Through his efforts to heal her, Ciyrs, the healer of the clan, had somehow changed her from a human into a Denynso woman. Though she was still small and delicate looking compared to the other women of their kind, she was truly one of them.

The other women had come in turn after her, each with her own reason for visiting the planet, and when they came they found themselves the chosen mates of Denynso men. Their courage to stay on the planet and be with the Denynso was already impressive. It was the incredible intelligence, strength, fortitude, and resourcefulness that they had shown that proved to Bannack that he and the others had been wrong. Of course, they were still far smaller than the Denynso, even Zuri and Samira, the two largest of the group, and were far more emotional as a whole than his kind, but they were also the central reason that the warriors had been able to dominate over the Klimnu in this final battle. It was these human women that found the mirror world, helped develop healing ointments that saved the wounded, and even fought alongside the warriors to enable their victory.

Bannack looked at the human women, and at Eden, her belly swollen with Pyra's child, the first of the new generation of Denynso, with respect and gratitude, but even these comforting feelings were not enough to dampen the fury and aggression that had been tormenting him since they dropped down from the moss-hidden holes in the forest into the mirror world beneath the compound. This was anger and intensity like he had never experienced, and he struggled with understanding what could be creating these feelings inside him when the other warriors didn't seem anywhere near as affected by the battle, or even by Jem's death, as he was. Though they had all expressed their own dark and painful emotions, they all seemed composed and controlled.

Soon Bannack couldn't take it anymore.

## 3

Bannack could hear the warriors behind him shouting as he broke out of their formation and started back toward the compound. He just couldn't stand there with the rest of the warriors anymore. He couldn't stand there and look at the kneeling women, the stoic king and queen, and the confused, hurting human women. He couldn't stand there and stare into the purple water, part of him waiting for Jem to simply swim to the edge and climb up out of it with his usual smile on his face, the funeral rite and the funnel of water somehow resurrecting him from his resting place in the reflected sky and allowing him to return to their number. He needed to get away.

He continued into the compound, picking up speed as he went so that he could put the lake and the entire ritual behind him as fast as he could. The emotions churning through him were too dark and too difficult for him to cope with, and he felt like he was losing control. Deep down, however, he knew that this was not all about Jem, or the battle. There was something else at play and it was pushing him ever forward toward the brink of his control over himself. He didn't know what was pushing him or how far he could go, but the thought of what may exist just beyond that threshold of control scared him.

"Bannack!" Pyra yelled from behind him as Bannack made it back into the center of the compound.

Bannack stopped and turned to face the other warriors as they streamed through the compound and joined him. He knew they were going to be angry with him. Leaving a funeral like that was not only extremely disrespectful to the fallen warrior, but to the rest of the tribe that relied on every member to band together during these difficult times and offer each other as much strength and support as possible.

"What?" he demanded as the massive, powerful warrior approached him.

"What the hell do you think you are doing storming out of the funeral like that?" Pyra shouted at him.

"I couldn't just stand there anymore, Pyra. With everything that just happened yesterday, how can we just stay goodbye to Jem and honor his death, and then move on like nothing happened? Like just because the Klimnu are gone, everything is perfectly fine and we should just go about our lives all happy and wonderful."

"What else would you want us to do, Bannack? The Klimnu are gone. The threat is over. It is horrible that Jem had to give his life for that to happen, but any of us would have. He sacrificed himself so that we could continue on with a future that isn't filled with all of the fear and pain and battles that they have put us through over the generations. We owe it to him to acknowledge what he did and honor him by continuing on with our lives."

"Pretending that there is nothing else that could threaten us is not honoring Jem, or anything that the rest of us went through. Jem is not the only one that suffered. We all put ourselves through brutality and pain to protect the clan and the compound. Now you just want us to think that that was it, that the Klimnu are all that could possibly ever want to get in our way or take over our land. What about the mirror world where Jem died? Can you explain that?"

Pyra fell silent and Bannack could see him stiffen. The warriors didn't want to think about that anymore. They didn't want to think about the strange, unexplainable place that none of them knew existed just beneath their feet, and what it could mean for them. Bannack saw Pyra look over his shoulder at the king and queen, who were approaching them quietly, their faces showing that they were as curious about what the warriors had gone through during the battle as Bannack was eager to talk about it and try to figure everything out.

"Is this the mirror world that the women told us about?" Creia asked.

Pyra nodded.

"We haven't heard very much about it."

"Tell them," Bannack demanded, "If you are so sure that there is nothing else to fear now that the Klimnu are gone, why don't you tell Creia, Theia, and the women about what we saw when we were down there?"

He wasn't used to standing up to Pyra like this, and usually he would expect for the head warrior to react strongly, even violently, but Bannack didn't care. He was tired of feeling like he was crawling within his own skin and that he was being ignored. It seemed ridiculous to him that they were all so willing to think that just because they had gotten rid of one source of threat in their lives that there would be nothing else. To him, the battle was only the beginning.

"I'm willing to talk about it," Pyra said slowly.

Creia nodded and turned to the others, who waited several feet away, not knowing what they should do. Eden stood slightly in front of the others, one hand rested over her growing belly protectively as she stared at her mate as if she could control his behavior just by staring intently at his back.

"Those who wish to know what the warriors and our brave human women experienced in the battle may come into the meeting hall with us and hear. Those who are not interested are welcome to go home and do what they please until dinnertime."

There were a few seconds where it seemed that the other warriors, the Denynso women, and the human women seemed to contemplate within themselves, and then with each other, whether they wanted to join in on the conversation about the battle. Some seemed to immediately know that they wanted to know what had happened. Others drifted toward the back of the center of the compound, drawn toward their homes where they could put the mourning behind them and continue forward in the Klimnu-free future that they had dreamed of for their entire lives.

Finally Bannack turned and climbed the stairs into the building, letting the others fall into step behind him. He walked into the main room of the meeting hall and took his place at one of the long tables positioned around the center of the room. Most of the other warriors, all of the human women, and a few of the Denynso women, along with the king and queen, made their way in after them and joined him at the tables.

"Tell us what happened," Theia said as the last person settled into place at the table.

They all had their eyes focused on Bannack, but he turned his gaze to Pyra. No matter what type of anger, frustration, and aggression he was experiencing, he knew that it was his position to respect Pyra. He had already stepped out of line so far that he deserved severe punishment, and it was time now that he relented and resumed the position chosen for him, which meant handing over the control of telling the story of the battle to Pyra.

"Do you remember when Zuri, Samira, and the other women went into the cave and discovered the tunnel that led down to the strange world that they described, where they saw the Klimnu?" Pyra started.

Everyone at the table nodded.

"Of course. That's why you created the battle plan as you did in the first place."

Pyra nodded in return and continued forward, describing the holes in the forest floor that were covered by moss, concealing them, explaining how they used the vines in the trees to attack the Klimnu, and recounting again the last horrific moments of Jem's life. Though Jem had gone into his death courageously, and even joyfully, it had been a crushing moment for everyone that was there. It was especially difficult for Ty, who had tried so hard to save him and who had made the decision to honor Jem's wishes and release him so that he could perform his final feat of heroism.

"Tell us what you're thinking, Bannack," Pyra said.

Bannack looked up and realized that everyone at the table was staring at him. He didn't know how long it had been since Pyra had stopped talking. He had been staring at the dark surface of the table, letting the images of the mirror world cross over his eyes again and again. He couldn't fight them, so he relinquished his mind to them, allowing himself to review them over and over so that he could clarify the details and commit them solidly to memory.

"Who made that mirror world? Was it the Klimnu, or did they steal it like they wanted to steal our compound?"

**4**

———

Bannack's words seemed to stun the others sitting at the table and he met their eyes carefully. He wanted what he had said to sink in and for them to really think about it. It had been something that he had been thinking about constantly since they first realized that the Klimnu were using the underground realm to infiltrate the compound. It seemed to him that if the Klimnu had had that capacity to create such an incredible, complex space, they would have had been able to put more into their attacks on the Denynso. It didn't make sense to him that a species that had spent generations so devoted to capturing Creia and taking down the entire clan, and who were known for their sparse, rough lifestyle would have put forth the effort to build something so strange, but so beautiful. It struck him as much more likely that the creatures had done what was in their nature and simply taken what they wanted rather than making it for themselves.

"How much do you know about the rest of the planet, Creia?"

The king looked older and more weathered in that

moment than Bannack had ever seen him. He didn't know if it was from the strain and stress of the battle or the realization that the peaceful future that he had dreamed of for so long was not yet guaranteed for them.

"Nothing," the king admitted, "The Denynso have been here for the entire existence of our kind. Our home has always been here. The compound has expanded since then, but it has been as it is now for as long as I can remember, and likely well before that."

"So you don't know what other types of creatures might live on Uoria?" Pyra asked.

The tremendous warrior suddenly seemed shaken. He stared at Creia with an expression on his face that seemed at once dismayed, let down, and angry. Bannack could understand exactly what he was feeling. Creia was a powerful and mighty king, one that they followed with absolute loyalty and devotion. He had been on the throne for longer than any of them had been alive, and was, in fact, the father of many of the warriors. To think that he had lived on that compound for his entire life without ever knowing what lay beyond it was disappointing and disheartening.

"It is our tradition to fight only those who threaten us. We have battled with species that have come from other planets, we have fought the Klimnu, and we have struggled against ourselves at times. There has never been the need to venture far out of our compound or to interact with any of the others that may occupy Uoria."

Pyra straightened and Bannack could see the darkness and anger roll over his eyes.

"How have you allowed us to not know what's beyond our compound? The unknown is what made the Klimnu such a brutal force, and what almost allowed them to defeat us. The entire planet is unknown to us. What if there are other creatures who know that we are here and want to come after us?"

"There has never been a threat, Pyra," Creia said sternly, speaking to his son with the tone of both a father and a king.

"Every threat comes after a time when there has been no threat."

Pyra seemed to be fighting to control himself. The anger was building inside him with such force it was visible. Eden reached out a hand and rested it on her mate's arm, looking at him with eyes that pled for him to stay calm.

"Are you questioning my choices as king?" Creia asked, the tone of his voice like a warning.

"I am questioning your decision, as someone who has been the primary focus of the violence and strategic attacks of the Klimnu, to pretend that there couldn't be other threats existing outside the compound. You say that our people have battled creatures from other planets. Why have we been so quick to wage war against species that come from other places in the galaxy, when we don't know anything about the species that live right on our own planet?"

There were several long, tense seconds and the look on Creia's face went from anger to regret.

"I wanted to do as all of the leaders before me have done, and I wanted to do what I thought was right for my people and my family. Staying in and near the compound meant staying safe. If we stayed here, we didn't cause trouble with the others that inhabit the planet. To me, that seemed to reduce the chances that we would be in danger."

"But we are warriors. We are known around the galaxy for that."

"Just because we can go to war, Pyra, doesn't mean that

we always have to. I didn't want to watch my children face any dangers that they didn't have to."

Pyra looked at Eden and then back at Creia.

"I am going to have a child of my own soon. I don't want that child born into a world that I don't understand. I have heard about the threat of the Klimnu my entire life. They have been looking for you for as long as I know. They're gone now, but how do I protect my child if I don't even know what I should be protecting him from?"

The mention of his grandchild, the first of the new generation, seemed to change something in Creia. He looked at Eden with painful softness in his eyes. She carried the hope of the future of their kind, and in that moment Bannack could see Creia shift. He couldn't let anything happen to that baby, and that meant finding out what threats could be lurking just outside the compound.

"Start with the mirror world," Creia said, his voice returning to his usual strong, steady tone, "Find out what you can about it. Find out if there are any species that live there, and then report back here. We will decide what to do about the rest of the planet from there."

Without another word, the warriors stood and started toward the door. Zuri, Samira, and Elianna followed closely behind, determined to return to where they had joined in the battle alongside their mates. Eden stayed behind, knowing that Pyra would never allow her to do something as dangerous as wander into an unknown area that had already claimed the life of one of their warriors when she was as far into her pregnancy as she was, and Leia stayed to be with her.

.   .   .

THE WARRIORS KNEW that they would not be able to get down the tunnel in the cave, so they would have to go down into the mirror realm in the same way that they did before the battle. They walked through the compound toward the forest in silence. Bannack could feel the tension among them and knew that they felt the same way that he did. None of them wanted to go back to the site of the battle so soon.

When they got to the forest, Bannack watched as Ero and Pyra pulled away the layers of moss that covered the holes leading down into the mirror realm beneath the compound. Moving slowly and carefully, they climbed down one by one. Bannack followed Pyra, grabbing onto one of the dangling vines as soon as he got deep enough. He wrapped the vine tightly around his wrist and forearm to secure him, and swung over so that he could grab onto the tree.

He concentrated on each of his movements, going slowly and carefully to keep himself from tumbling down toward the bright blue reflection of the sky that looked even more like water rippling across the ground of the massive cavern. Bannack looked up and watched the rest of the warriors make their way down the trees. The human women were last, coming down even more gradually than their warriors due to their smaller size. The warriors watched them intently, ready to catch them if they stumbled. Once they made it all the way down, they gripped onto their mates, holding them closely both to keep themselves steady on the branches that stretched out across the sky and to gain strength and comfort from their presence.

As Bannack looked around, he felt the fury and aggression that had eased slightly roar back into full intensity. His stomach clenched and he felt a strange pressure building throughout his pelvis and down his thighs. He struggled against the feeling, fighting to focus on what Pyra was saying even though his voice seemed to be coming through fog at him. Bannack tightened his grip around the vines, hoping that the pain of the thick plant cutting into his palm would turn his focus from the feelings building inside him. Around him the warriors were strategizing about how to safely and effectively explore the cavern, but all Bannack could think about was the intense, almost irresistible pull he felt toward the back corner.

## 5

I sank as deeply down into the shadows as I could while still being able to see the Denynso and the women I assumed to be the human females that had joined their tribe. The fear coursed through me so powerfully that I felt like I couldn't catch my breath and I struggled to hold myself silent as I watched them. I had, of course, seen them before. They had been there only the day before when they had descended from the moss and struck down the pale, disgusting creatures that had been crawling through my home for many months.

I didn't think that any of them noticed that I was there. Just like during the battle, I stayed out of sight, keeping completely to myself so that they didn't know that I even existed. That was the way that I liked it, the way that it had been for several years since the rest of my kind succumbed to an illness so severe that it burned through our families in a matter of days and killed everyone that it touched. I had no idea why it spared me. There have been many times when I wished that it hadn't. It would have been much simpler to let it take me as it had everyone that I knew and loved. Instead, it left me with the memory of youngest sister disappearing into the sky as I let her slip through my fingers.

The creatures that live on the ground above me have never known that we were here. My grandmother once told me that our kind didn't always live in this cavern. We once lived where the Denynso have settled, but a brutal war with another species and a plague that threatened our very existence drove us down into the cavern, a space that the wisest and most powerful of our species living then transformed into a reflection of the land above, the land that our clan loved so deeply. They had no way of knowing that the plague followed us down. It would be many generations before it struck again, but when it did it did so with a vengeance and only I was left behind.

Now I was more alone than I could ever imagine that a person could be. I was not just the last of my kind, the last of my family and friends. I was the last of a species that had been out of sight for so long that no other species on the planet even remembered that we existed. If anything, I was a myth and a legend.

I could see the men clutching their vines tightly as they scanned the reflection of the sky that covered all of the floor of the cavern that they could see. They all emanated fear and uncertainty, emotions that none of them were accustomed to feeling, and that none of them wanted to admit to the others. They all hated to feel as though there was something that they didn't understand so close to a space that they only knew as their own. The human women were more difficult for me to decipher. Unlike the warriors, who presented themselves as cold as stone on their exteriors but in fact presented their thoughts and feelings quite readily, the women held themselves closer, protecting themselves with their own internal forces so that I had to concentrate intently on each of them to be able to see what they were experiencing inside.

Many times I had heard the legends of the Denynso warriors and their incredible might, both on the battlefield and with their mates. It was said that these massive, forceful men fought with more intensity, skill, aggression, and determination than any other creature that had ever existed among the stars, but when they found their mate, they could be tamed as quickly as a pet. The warriors went through a difficult change when they neared their mate, struggling with their anger, primal force, and arousal until their mate soothed them. The blazing heat of their skin kept all but their intended partner away from them, and once they bonded, it was permanent. I had been told that these partners shared a very special gift that enabled them to communicate with each other through their minds even when they were far apart.

I often wished that my abilities were like that. I didn't read the minds of those I saw. Instead, I looked into them and reflected back to them the essence of who they were; their thoughts, their feelings, and their struggles. Now I was struggling myself, trying to grip what the human women were experiencing as they watched the warriors slowly and carefully extricate themselves from the vines and start to make their way out onto the branches that snaked and intersected across the sky. It was those branches that were perhaps the most brilliant element of the creation of that ancestor of our kind. He designed the cavern so that it reflected the space our species knew as its home so that we could always remember what the land looked like, but with that design came protection.

Those that made their way down into our cavern would

see the branches and walk out onto them, thinking that they could make their way across the entirety of the cavern. The branches would only go so far, though, and just like the ones on the ground above, some were weak and could snap in an instant, sending whoever stood upon it tumbling into the unknown beyond the sky. There had been very few who had ventured down to the cavern in recent generations, and none in my lifetime until the Klimnu appeared. When they did, it was the first time that I had been truly thankful for the illness that had taken everyone else. Their deaths had been fast, and though it left me alone, I would have much preferred that to watching my family and loved ones go through the horrors I could only imagine those creatures would have inflicted on us if they had found our colony thriving.

As I watched them, one of the men caught my attention. He was not the largest of the group and he, like the others, were definitely under the control and guidance of the tremendous one that now stepped out onto one of the biggest branches and hunched down to stabilize himself as he made his way out a few feet over the sky. There was something about him, though, that made me not want to turn away. His hair was stark white like the hair of the rest of the warriors, but unlike them, who wore their hair in high, spiky mohawks, his was tightly braided down his back and tied with a stretch of dark fabric. I remembered seeing him in the battle the night before. He had been much the same then, exuding an energy that was wild, unchained, and volatile despite being contained within his quiet exterior.

He looked up in my direction and for a brief moment I thought that he might be able to see me. I sank back further into the shadows and watched him narrow his eyes, the energy within him send out aggressive, powerful waves that drew me in even more. Part of me wanted to reach out to them, to tell them about the cavern and unveil its secrets, but the other part was so frightened and unsure of them that I couldn't move from my spot.

The man I had been watching stepped forward onto one of the branches and my heart tightened. I knew that he had chosen one of the weaker branches and the further he stepped, the more likely he was to fall. Keeping my eyes focused on him, I crept out from behind the low hill where I had been hiding. I lifted my hand to my chest as I made my way quickly, but as quietly as I could, toward the very edge of the bank where the land on this side of the cavern would flow into the sky. They couldn't see me where I was standing. They thought that the sky filled the entire space. Knowing that made me feel more secure, but even if they had suspected that there was something beyond the gradually darkening sky, I wouldn't have stopped.

The man took another step and I heard the low creak of the wood. The growing darkness of the sky was making it more difficult for him to differentiate between the branch and the sky, and he took another step onto one of the smaller outshoots of the branch. He stumbled and I heard a gasp rise out of the human women. One of the warriors started toward him, but I acted first. I tore my necklace from my neck, opening the compact in my hand and thrusting it forward. As the reflection of the stone wall across from me came into view on the bottom portion of the mirrored compact I stepped forward into the sky.

**6**

———

Bannack heard the sickening sound before he felt the branch beneath his feet crack. Pyra yelled behind him and he heard the women scream. For just a moment the world slowed down and a wave of peace washed over him as if everything around him had gone quiet and calm, and his body could release. Maybe this is what Jem had felt in those seconds before he jumped.

An instant later he felt his body fall forward and he knew that he was going to drop into the sky and discover whatever existed beyond. The branch disappeared from beneath his feet and he felt his body straighten, but it didn't drift downward. Instead, there was a brief moment of falling before he hit something hard and solid. It was as though he had tripped and landed on the hard packed earth and stone of the cliffs, only harder. The impact took the breath out of him, but he didn't feel any pain. He lay still, waiting for something, anything to happen.

Chaos broke around him as the other warriors ran toward him and scooped him up, dragging him back toward the trees before he could even get his feet beneath him. The women were talking so quickly that he couldn't understand any of the words that they were saying. His mind was reeling. He was aware that he hadn't fallen into the sky like he had expected to even though the branch had broken beneath him, but he had no idea what had actually happened. Suddenly he noticed a faint, pearlescent glow across the cavern. His eyes locked on it and he felt the muscles of his stomach clench. His pants tightened painfully and a wave of confusion rolled over him.

Bannack released the vine he was gripping and took a step toward the edge of the trees again, wanting to get closer to the glow. When it didn't fade or disappear, he took another step toward it. He felt Pyra's hand grab the back of his tunic and try to pull him back, but he lifted his hand to wave him away. He didn't need to be rescued. He wanted to be near the glow and whatever was making it. Though he knew he was only inches away from the edge of the sky, he believe he would be fine when he stepped forward. There was no fear as he lifted his foot away from the trunk and stepped out into the darkness.

His foot again hit solid ground rather than the sky and the confidence built inside him. The validation of that first step propelled him forward and he took another. He could hear Pyra and the other warriors protesting behind him, but the human women argued with their mates, telling them not to follow him. Bannack didn't care whether they followed or not. He continued to walk toward the glow, knowing each time he took a step that the solid ground would be there to meet his feet. As he walked the glow grew brighter and more intense, and soon he realized that there was a figure within the light.

"Hello?" he called out softly as he approached.

There was no response, but he continued forward still. The figure became more defined as he got closer and he realized that it was not actually within the glow but behind it. It seemed to move away from him, but he wasn't worried. He took another step, allowing the slowly retreating glow to lead him forward toward the other side of the cavern. After a few more steps he felt the texture of the ground beneath him change from hard and solid to slightly softer and more resilient. As soon as his feet touched that surface, the bright glow disappeared and out of the corner of his eye he could see the floor behind him go from solid and dark back to a sky awash with stars and a vibrant full moon.

Bannack turned his attention back to where the glow had been and found a woman standing in front of him. The figure that had been standing behind the glow, she was emanating her own very soft light that didn't seem to be coming from within her, but off of her. She wore a long white dress that gently skimmed the lines of her body and stopped with a band across her chest so the soft upper swells of her breasts and her smooth, elegant shoulders were bare. Ties down the front of the dress held it just in place, making the dress and what lie beneath even more intriguing. Pale silver hair flowed to her knees and the eyes that stared back at him from a face so breathtakingly beautiful it didn't seem real, her eyes were a clear, hypnotic lavender. She closely resembled the human women, but it was obvious that she wasn't.

Without a word, she held out one slim, graceful hand and Bannack took it, resting his hand on top so that she could curl her fingers around his coarser skin and draw him closer to her. The nearer he got to her, the more intense the feelings that he had as soon as he stepped into the cavern became, only he was no longer feeling anger or aggression when he was near her. Instead, he felt a sense of power and calm, while the tension through his body seemed to only increase.

"Hello," he said, wanting to make more of a connection with the beautiful creature standing so quietly and calmly in front of him.

"Hello," she replied and her voice was like the delicate, dancing sound of raindrops hitting glass. "Are you alright?"

"Yes," Bannack replied, somewhat startled by the question.

She didn't seem to be asking about whether he had been injured, and the question cut deeply into him.

"My name is Loralia," she said.

"Bannack," he replied.

He realized that she was still holding his hand and despite the cool feeling of her skin, the touch sent warmth throughout his body. She smiled at him softly, but he couldn't decipher what was behind the smile.

"Would your friends like to come to this side of the cavern?" she asked.

"I don't even know how I got over here," Bannack replied, part of him not wanting them to come over and break the small circle of privacy that surrounded them because of their distance from the others.

"I can help them." Loralia released his hand and Bannack felt disappointment ripple through him. "It's alright," she said with a gentle laugh, glancing at him before stepping forward toward the edge of the sky, "I'm right here."

It was as if she knew what he was feeling even though he hadn't said anything, but her confirmation was soothing in a way that made him feel absolutely comfortable and secure. She turned her palm over and in the faint light coming off of her skin and the refraction from the moon he saw what looked like a silver compact in her palm. Loralia held her palm out in front of her and lifted the top of the compact. Immediately the bright glow filled the space again and Bannack realized that the inside of both sides of the compact was mirrored. She tilted the compact until the stone wall across the cavern came into view in the top mirror.

The alignment of the bottom mirror made it so that it reflected the image in the top mirror, showing the wall flat against her palm.

"It's safe now," she called out, her voice so gentle and quiet that Bannack wasn't sure if the others would hear her.

Just as he suspected, none of the warriors or the human women stepped forward.

"She says it's safe," he called out to them.

They looked back at him with uncertainty on their faces, so Bannack took a few steps forward, leaving the softer ground of the bank and stepping again onto the hard, solid ground of the sky. He knew it was going to be there without even looking down.

Bannack taking those few steps seemed enough to convince Zuri, who took let go of Ero and took one large step forward, forgoing easing out over the space and instead going right for an open expanse between two branches. Samira followed, taking a slightly more cautious step, but stopping just beside Zuri. Bannack knew that the warriors not stepping forward was not out of fear, but out of distrust. Finally the men started forward and soon everyone was walking calmly across the expanse toward Bannack.

Suddenly he heard a scream and a deep grunt. He looked toward the back of the group and saw Ciyrs holding Elianna up by her arm as she struggled, her legs kicking down through a small section of the floor that now showed the sparkle of the stars rather than the solid darkness from before.

7

———

My stomach sank as I watched the tiny human woman drop, but she had had enough of a grip on the Denynso beside her that he was able to catch her before she was lost. Terror rolled over me. If her falling made any of the other ones question the solidity of the ground beneath their feet, they, too, would begin falling. Instead, they all rushed forward, getting off of the expanse of reflected stone as quickly as they could and then turning angry, suspicious eyes toward me.

"What the hell do you think you're doing?" the man that had rescued the small woman who fell demanded, taking an aggressive step toward me.

He didn't feel like a warrior. He seemed gentler, calmer, more nurturing despite his attempt to intimidate me.

"Ciyrs," the woman said, grabbing him and pulling him back, "You don't know that she did anything."

I felt relief wash over me. At least this one seemed to be willing to trust me rather than immediately blaming me.

"What do you think happened, Elianna?" another of the warriors snapped toward the small woman, "She's the one that told us it was all of a sudden safe to walk on the sky, and then as soon as you do, you fall."

"Don't talk to my mate like that," Ciyrs snarled toward the warrior, turning his aggression to him instead of me.

"I'm just pointing out that it's ridiculous for her to defend this person, whoever she is, when she is obviously the one who just tried to kill her."

Suddenly everyone started talking and shouting over top of one another and I felt like I was filling with so many feelings, emotions, and energies that I was going to shatter. I held my hands up and shouted as loudly as I could possibly force my voice.

"Stop it! All of you."

The cavern fell silent and the group turned and looked at me. Bannack seemed startled, but somewhat pleased, at my outburst and he stepped a little closer to me.

"What is it?" he asked.

"I didn't try to kill her," I said, wanting to talk to the entire group but at the same time feeling the compulsion to talk only to him, "It wasn't my fault."

"Then whose fault is it?" Ciyrs demanded.

"Hers," I said matter-of-factly.

"What?" he said roughly and I noticed all of the warriors looking at him with surprised looks on their faces as if he never showed this type of personality toward anyone.

Indeed, I could see the healer within him and knew that this was not in his normal nature. When it came to his mate, however, he was far more intense and aggressive than he would ever be when he was away from her. This made me less angry at the way he had treated me, but I was still not happy.

"In order for a reflection to mean anything, you have to believe in that reflection. If you didn't know what an item was and you saw a reflection of it, you still would not know what it was. You wouldn't embrace its presence and believe in its functions because you wouldn't know about them. If you looked in a mirror and saw something that you thought was something else, you would still believe that that reflection was what you thought it was and that if it was real, it would function the way you expected it to. Reflections only have the meaning that you give them. If you don't believe in the reflection, it can't work for you. She didn't believe in the stone beneath her feet, so the stone was no longer there."

I expected for them to react strongly again, but they surprised me by seeming to accept what I had told them without further argument. Even if they had argued, there would be nothing else that I could have said to them. It was a very simple concept, though one that may be difficult to grasp for those who hadn't grown up with such rules governing their existence.

"Do you live here?" the largest of the warriors asked me.

"Yes."

"May we look around?"

It was an unusual moment, a moment of balance and control. This was a moment that I had been waiting on for years, a moment when I would no longer be alone and could possibly look forward into a life that was not isolated beneath the ground for the majority of the time, and yet a moment that I also feared. I was so accustomed to being alone and to protecting the space that had once been the home to everyone who I have ever loved that it was frightening to me in a way to think of others entering the deeper areas of the space. I was very aware that nearly every inch of the land ground was a place where someone I cared for had taken their last step or even their last breath, and I had the irrational fear that if these people stepped on those places, they would cover them and diminish the memory of those last moments.

I glanced over at Bannack and found him looking at me, evaluating me. Looking at him offered me a sense of anchoring among the others in a way that I didn't understand. It was as though the rest of the group and I were completely separate entities, but that Bannack could act as a link between us that would close the space.

"Yes," I finally said, offering my permission for them to go further into the cavern.

"This is Loralia," Bannack introduced.

"Hello, Loralia. My name is Pyra."

One by one the warriors and the women introduced themselves to me and I found myself attaching characteristics to each of their names so that I would remember them more clearly later. Zuri was incredibly strong, but adored the way that her mate made her feel feminine and beautiful. Samira held wounds that were still healing, but for the first time in her life, she felt like she belonged. Elianna was vibrant and spirited, but still had a vulnerability in her that seemed to come from an event in the recent past that shaped her now and for the future.

I nodded at each of them as they introduced themselves and tried to offer smiles that would comfort them and ease their worries about me. Once everybody was introduced, Pyra started forward, keeping his eyes trained on me as he moved further into the cavern. There was still a heavy sense of distrust around him as he moved slowly past me and then ventured deeper. The others followed him, gazing around as they moved beyond the hill where I had been hiding when they first entered and stepped down into the expansive chamber that dipped lower and contained the first collection of small buildings that were once home to my friends and family. Two tunnels led off of this chamber, each leading to another chamber containing more buildings.

Off of these chambers were two more tunnels that fed together into one narrow corridor that led deep into the cavern to the chamber that our kind used as its greatest source of protection. When there were threats, we would gather there, utilizing our mirrors to reflect a solid wall over the mouth of the cavern so that no one could enter. I spent much of my time there, forgoing the home I once shared with my parents and siblings to live in the protecting surroundings of this nearly empty chamber.

"There is a tunnel that leads off of that first room and goes up into the cliffs at the edge of our compound," Pyra said.

It seemed more a statement than a question, but I replied anyway.

"Yes. I haven't used it in many years."

"Are there any other tunnels that lead into the cavern from above ground?"

"No. The only way to enter is that tunnel and the hatches in the forest."

"How often do you go above ground?"

The change in voice made me turn to Bannack, who was still standing close beside me. There was a faintly desperate look in his eyes and I could feel the sense that he was trying to understand of the emotions rolling through him, as if knowing how often I walked on the same ground as he did.

"Never," I told him, keeping my voice as even and calm as I could in an effort to assure him.

"How do you survive down here without ever going up?"

"The cavern provides everything that I need. There are plants throughout the cavern and a stream in the middle chamber. I was born down here and have always been here."

"Will you come up with us now?"

My eyes widened and I saw Pyra look sharply at Bannack, but he didn't say anything. My warrior, for that is how I was beginning to think of him, was staring at me intently and I saw him lift his hand toward me.

I hesitated only a moment before placing my fingers against the warmth of his palm and seeing the hint of a smile touch his lips.

8

———

Bannack wrapped his hand around Loralia's fingers as soon as he felt their cool touch on his palm and turned to Pyra.

"We said that we wanted to learn more about the other species that are on this planet. Why don't we let her tell us?"

Pyra agreed and they started back toward the front of the cavern, allowing Loralia to use her compact to change the glimmering night sky spread across the floor into the hardened stone of the wall so that they could walk across it. Just like he had since the first time he had walked toward her, Bannack believed completely in the safety of the ground beneath his feet and crossed without hesitation, his hand cradling Loralia's beside him. The others paused briefly at the edge and Bannack saw them take a few breaths as if preparing themselves and convincing themselves that the ground would be solid when they stepped forward.


"Where are the others of your kind?"

Loralia looked up at Creia where he sat on his massive

throne without flinching. Bannack found himself watching her in awe, admiring how she could go from an underground realm she had always known to facing the king of an above ground species without showing any sign of intimidation or fear.

"There are no others," Loralia told him calmly, "I am the last of my kind."

"What happened to them?"

"There was a plague several years ago. I am the only one to survive."

Whispers rippled through the meeting hall and Bannack turned to glare at the others, suddenly protective and defensive. He knew that no matter how Loralia was handling herself in that moment as she faced down the king, confronting a strange species that was far larger and more powerful than her, and that she had always heard were the ones who had taken over the land her kind had once inhabited after war and illness drove them underground, had to be frightening to her. He didn't want the reaction of the rest of the Denynso to upset her further.

Bannack turned his attention back to Creia, who looked at his wife in a way that told Bannack that the mates were communicating silently. Theia turned to Loralia and he saw the gentle, nurturing look in her eyes that made her the mother figure of all of the Denynso.

"You are welcome here, Loralia," she said warmly, "You may stay with us for as long as you would like."

Bannack wasn't sure how Loralia was going to react, but he saw her take the few steps up toward the platform where the thrones sat and reach her pale, lovely hands toward the queen. Theia stood from her throne and approached Loralia as if she were as drawn to her as Bannack felt, and took the beautiful woman's hands in hers.

"Thank you."

Loralia's voice was so gentle Bannack could barely hear it, but he felt a little jump in his heart when he realized that she had accepted the queen's invitation to stay. The conflict he felt when he looked at her was so intense it made his stomach twist painfully. As much as he wanted to be near her, and the intense way his body responded whenever he looked at her, he was still extremely aware that she was a completely different, unknown species. He knew nothing about her or her kind, and part of him was still extremely wary about getting close to her.

Bannack jumped when he felt a heavy hand land on his shoulder. He looked up to see Ero standing beside him.

"What are you thinking about so hard over here?" the other warrior asked.

"Her," Bannack said, nodding toward Loralia, "How is it possible that she has been living right underneath us her entire life and not only did we not know she was there, we didn't even know that there was a place for anything to live down there? From what she said, her species has been down there since long before the Denynso even existed. We have lived right over top of her kind for generations, but there was never any interaction."

"So?"

"So? Doesn't that make you suspicious? If they have been down there that whole time, they would know when the Denynso settled. Why did they just stay down there and not come up and try to make contact?"

"Maybe they didn't feel like they had any reason to. There was never any conflict, so why shake things up? Isn't existing peacefully what matters?"

Bannack looked back at Loralia.

"I don't know. It just seems weird to me. I don't know how I feel about her staying around here."

"You are the one that quite literally took her by the hand and brought her here. Why did you do that if you didn't want her here?"

Bannack sighed.

"I don't know," he answered honestly, "I just felt like it was what I should do in that moment."

Ero looked at him and Bannack saw his mouth twitch like he was fighting a smile. The other warrior nodded and his eyes traveled briefly down Bannack's body.

"Yep," Ero said, patting Bannack on the back, "I'm sure you did."

Ero walked away, heading back across the meeting hall toward Zuri. Confused, Bannack glanced down and saw exactly what had called Ero's amused attention to the lower half of his body. Muttering expletives under his breath, Bannack tried to adjust himself as quickly and subtly as he could to make his raging erection less obvious. Just as he was finishing, he saw Creia look up at him and gesture for him to come to the platform. By now both the king and queen were standing at the edge of the platform and as Bannack approached he saw them grin happily at him.

"I hear you have met our new friend," Creia said, reaching out to touch his hand to Bannack's shoulder.

"Yes," Bannack replied.

"She has accepted our invitation to stay with us and she requested that you be her guide and protector while she is here."

Bannack looked over at Loralia and found her gazing back at him, the lavender of her eyes so intoxicating he felt like he was falling into them. He felt her hand intertwine with his again and his erection twitched. The frustration and confusion built inside him and he felt painfully torn. He knew that he couldn't deny the king and queen his service as her protector, but the way his heart and body were responding to him made him feel both excited and repelled. She was at once the most beautiful and intriguing creature that he had ever seen, and something that made him uncomfortable.

"I will," he answered.

"Good. Bring her to the house where Samira was going to live," Creia turned back to Loralia, "I hope that you will be comfortable there."

"I'm sure I will," Loralia responded, "Thank you for your kindness."

Bannack gave a nod toward the king and queen and led Loralia out of the meeting hall, forcing himself to keep his eyes trained forward rather than letting them wander over to her or to acknowledge the group of warriors sitting at one long table, watching him and muttering comments as they passed. He knew what they were saying, but he didn't want to acknowledge it.

Loralia took a deep breath as they stepped out of the building and into the quiet center of the compound.

"I love the way the air smells up here," she said, "It's so different from the cavern."

"I'm glad you like it," Bannack replied gruffly, not turning his eyes toward her.

Finally they arrived at the simple house on the same row as the other homes the Denynso reserved for the scientists and students who had been invited to visit Uoria as part of the exchange program. He opened the door for her and stepped back to allow her to enter in front of him.

"Will you come in with me?" she asked gently. Bannack hesitated. "It's the first night that I've spent away from the cavern in my entire life. I don't want to be alone just yet. Please just spend a few minutes with me."

No matter what he tried to tell himself, Bannack couldn't resist her request. He stepped forward into the house and let Loralia close the door behind him.

"The solar panels collect energy throughout the day so you can use the lights and heat water for a shower."

Bannack turned back to Loralia and saw her staring at him.

"Why are you fighting it?" she asked, taking a step toward him.

**9**

---

I could see the confusion flicker across his eyes, but the intense feelings were still radiating toward me as I walked slowly toward Bannack. His gaze traveled along me, exploring the curves and planes of my face and the dips of my body, but I could still sense the internal struggle that was keeping him from admitting what was coursing through his mind and his veins.

"Fighting what?" he finally asked me, his voice strained slightly.

"What you are feeling right now."

I was only two steps away from him now, close enough that I could feel intense, powerful heat pulsing off of his body and see the swell in the front of his loose-fitting pants.

"Can you read my thoughts?" he asked defensively, obviously uncomfortable with not only the concept that I would be able to get into his mind and read what was there, but what the implications of that ability would be if I was to be able to do it.

Still staring at the front of his pants, I bit my bottom lip and shook my head slowly, finally lifting my eyes to his.

"No," I said, "but I can sense what you're feeling. I can look into you and see and feel what is inside you. I know what you're thinking about right now, and I want to know why you are fighting it."

He didn't respond and I lifted my hands to the ties at the front of my dress. I released them slowly and carefully, deliberately looking into his eyes as I did. The ties stretched from my neckline down to the center of my stomach and I loosened them all the way down. Once the ties had fallen loose, the bodice of my dress slipped down, revealing my breasts. Bannack cleared his throat and looked away, but I didn't stop. I could feel my hair sweep across my bare back as I carefully pushed the dress down over my hips and let it pool at my feet. I was barefoot as I always was, so when I stepped out of the soft white fabric and gently kicked it aside, I was standing in front of Bannack in only a pair of thin, finely woven panties that tied at either hip.

"Why do you keep fighting?" I asked again, taking another step toward him so that only one more step separated us.

Bannack shifted where he stood, looking around as if he couldn't find something to rest his eyes on so that he didn't look at me.

"I can't feel this way about you," he finally said and I felt a little flicker in my belly.

"Feel what way about me?" I asked.

He looked at me and the confusion in his eyes had turned dark and mixed with the desire coursing through his body.

"You know exactly what way," he nearly snarled.

"Of course you can feel that way," I said.

"And why is it so easy for you to just say that?" he asked.

The tension in his voice said that he was being sarcastic, but at the same time he was truly asking me.

"Because," I said, taking hold of the strings on either side of my panties, "you already do."

I pulled the strings, releasing the ties and letting my panties fall free away from my body. I could feel what was inside him more intensely in that moment than I had in any other except for the very first moment when I saw him in the cavern. I had known immediately and the feeling building inside me was something that I had never experienced. The longer I looked at him, the more I realized that what I was feeling was not a matter of a simple reflection. I had fallen completely under his spell and I was helpless to resist him, even if he was trying to resist what he was feeling himself.

Bannack's eyes shifted briefly into a dark orange and I saw his hands clench, tightening into fists as if he was fighting to control his body as much as his mind. I closed the space between us with a final step, bringing us close enough that my breasts brushed against him and I could feel his erection straining toward me. I reached up and touched his cheek, guiding his face so that he looked down into my eyes. The pad of my thumb stroked over his lips and Bannack's eyes drifted closed. I could feel the breath stream from his lungs and ripple from the inside of my wrist down my arm. The warm feeling made my nipples tighten and I felt a tingle slip down between my thighs.

I walked around Bannack further into the house, making my way toward the furniture arranged in the middle of the main room. After a few steps, Bannack followed me. We didn't speak, but our hands expressed more than words could have in that moment. He approached me and I took the end of the tie that closed his pants in one hand. As I loosened it, my warrior cupped one of his hands around my breast and ran his thumb across my nipple, making it ache. His pants slipped down his hips to his feet and he stepped out of them and his soft boots at the same time. As he pulled his shirt off over his head, I rested my palm against his long, hard shaft and wrapped my fingers around it. I stroked him carefully but insistently, watching my hand in awe as it moved across his erection.

I felt his finger tuck under my chin and lift my face up to his. There was a still, quiet moment, and then he leaned forward to touch his lips to mine. The kiss filled me as if it gave me breath, satisfying something deep within me that I hadn't even known needed fulfillment until I saw him for the first time. Our mouths moved across each other languidly, tenderly and carefully discovering the feeling and taste of each other's lips and welcoming each other's tongues to slip between, tangling and exploring.

Bannack stepped forward, pushing me back so that he could turn and sit down in the large chair I had been standing beside. Our mouths parted and I could hear our heavy breaths filling the space around us, accentuating the silence we had maintained. Bannack's strong hands turned me and eased me back so that I sat on his lap, moving my hair aside so that it cascaded down his thing and along the front of the chair. His body cradled me, surrounding me in his warmth and the strength of his presence. He wrapped his arms around me and I let my head rest back against his shoulder.

We remained still for several long seconds, our breaths synchronizing as his heartbeat created an enticing yet comforting rhythm against my back. His hand flattened in the middle of my chest and smoothed its way down my body, pausing in the dip between my hipbones. I could feel myself trembling and my breath caught in my throat as he applied gentle pressure. No one's hands had ever touched me and I found myself overwhelmed with the sensation of his body so close to mine and his hand easing down between my thighs.

Bannack's other hand carefully parted my legs to give himself better access, keeping his grip on my thigh as if providing stability. The first touch of his fingers in the warmth of my body sent shockwaves through me and I cried out, arching off of him so that he took his hand way from my thigh and rested it on my belly, easing me back down into his lap. I let the strength of his hand on stomach relax and reassure me, and my body rested down against him. Releasing the tension in my thighs, I allowed my knees to fall open further and welcomed his touch. Bannack's fingers explored my hot, wet folds, building dizzying sensations and tension throughout my hips, thighs, and lower belly.

Suddenly the feelings shattered within me and a cascade of intense tremors rippled through my body. My hips lifted up out of his lap and I felt his strong, powerful erection slip from behind my back to in front of me. I tucked my hand around it, pressing it against my body so that he could feel the warm wetness that he created. Acting purely on instinct, I rolled my hips, letting my core run along his length until I could hear him groaning behind me. I wanted him inside me in a way that I had never wanted anything. I lifted my hips, readying myself to guide him to my entrance, when I felt Bannack's hands suddenly tighten on my hips.

"Stop."

**10**

———

Bannack held his shirt under his arm as he rushed out of Loralia's house, tying the strings on the front of his pants and trying to block her voice out of his ears. He could hear her behind him, shouting for him, calling for him to come back, but he forced the sound away and kept forging ahead, dropping his shirt down over his body and setting out at a run. The thoughts and emotions rushing through his mind had reached a fevered pitch when he felt the intoxicating, entrancing warmth of her body against him and he just couldn't let himself keep going. As much as he wanted her, and it was far more than he could ever have imagined wanting anyone or anything in his entire life, he hadn't been able to silence the conflicts and questions raging in his head.

"Bannack!"

A different voice forced itself into his consciousness and he paused to turn toward it. Ero was running toward him across the compound. Ero was always running. It was something that he had done since he was young to combat his own feelings and escape whatever was bothering him at the moment. He used to run out of fear and anger, but since he had found Zuri he ran only to amuse himself and when he was needed.

"What is it Ero?" he asked, the question coming out sharper and angrier than he had intended.

"Pyra told me to get all of the warriors in the meeting hall."

"For what?"

"I don't know. He seemed really serious about it, though."

"Does he know that Creia assigned me as Loralia's protector?"

"Why would that have anything to do with him wanting you at the meeting hall? Besides, if you are her protector, why aren't you with her?"

The question fell like a rock into Bannack's gut and he shook his head, trying to shake the images of the time he had just spent with the gorgeous, confounding creature. Ero seemed to know not to push the issue and the two warriors hurried toward the meeting hall in silence. When they got inside, the main room bustled with voices and an argument seemed to be going on at one of the long tables.

Suddenly Pyra jumped up onto the table so that he was visible above the heads of the other warriors and Denynso men who had gathered around him. Bannack looked around and saw Creia sitting silently on the platform, staring at the men with a look on his face that was at once worried and pleased.

"If you aren't brave enough to come with me, then don't," Pyra shouted and some of the warriors shouted back at him, "I'm going. The king has given me permission and I am going to take it. I've already discussed it with Eden, and she agrees that we don't want to bring our baby into this world until we know what kinds of threats, and what kinds of opportunities, may exist outside of our compound. She may be close to delivery, which means that I need to go soon if I am to be back by the time the baby arrives."

"Where are you going?" Bannack shouted up toward the warrior.

Pyra looked down at him.

"I'm going to explore Uoria outside of the compound. There are other species out there that we don't know anything about, and I want to change that. Eden, Leia, Elianna, Zuri, and Samira all came here from Earth because the humans want to know more about our kind, yet we haven't even gone so far as the other side of our own planet to find out what might be there."

"When are you leaving?"

"Three days. I need the time to get together all of the supplies that I might need while I'm gone." He straightened and looked out over the group of warriors. "Who's with me?"

There was defiance in his voice, a sense of strength and defensiveness that seemed to come from the idea that there were things he couldn't protect his mate and future child from because he didn't know what they were or what they might do. It enraged him, and as the fiercest and most aggressive of the warriors already, that was intimidating to see.

A few of the other warriors yelled back up to him, but Bannack turned and ran toward Creia's platform.

"Are you alright, Bannack?" the king asked as he approached.

"May I have permission to have a leave from my responsibilities to Loralia and go with the other warriors?" Bannack asked, ignoring Creia's question.

The king hesitated.

"She is new to our compound, Bannack. She specifically

asked if you would be her guide. That must mean that she trusts you."

"I understand that, but I feel that I would be better serving the tribe if I went with the warriors and helped explore the planet. I'm sure that the human women would be happy to keep an eye on Loralia and help her get accustomed to the compound. They would probably do better than me anyway."

"Why do you say that?"

"Because they're different, too."

"Different?"

The king seemed to be testing Bannack in some way, but he didn't have the patience to explore what he might mean.

"They aren't Denynso. They are a different kind, so they know what it's like to be a strange species among the tribe. It might make her feel better to spend some time with them."

"I'll give you permission to go with the warriors, Bannack, if you are able to convince the women to take on your role as protector. But listen carefully when I tell you to think about your decision, and your reasoning, carefully."

Bannack nodded his thanks and ran back across the meeting hall. He couldn't get the taste of Loralia's lips or the feeling of her body on his fingers out of his mind no matter how hard he found them, and he knew that he had to get to the women so that he could get them on his side and start preparing for the journey. He, like the other Denynso, had never ventured away from the compound, but right now getting as far away from his home, and from Loralia, as possible seemed like the only thing that he could do.

He got to the edge of the table where Pyra stood and shouted up at him over the voices of the other warriors who still seemed to be locked in a debate over whether they should go at all. Many thought that it would better serve them to concentrate on building up the defenses of the compound before they started searching for threats.

"Where's Eden?" Bannack asked.

"She's at the bakery with Samira. Why do you need her?"

"Creia says that the only way I can go with you is to get the human women to agree to watch over Loralia while I'm gone."

"Why?"

"She chose me as her protector."

A smile crossed Pyra's lips, but Bannack refused to acknowledge it. He pushed away from the table and ran out of the meeting hall toward the bakery. The smell of fresh, hot bread greeted him as soon as he opened the door.

"I need your help," he said and saw Eden jump slightly where she was sitting on a high stool near the counter where Samira was rolling out long ropes of dough to form into braided loaves.

"Is everything alright?"

"I want to go with the warriors to explore Uoria, but I need someone to watch Loralia while I'm gone. She chose me as her protector and guide, and the king says that I can only have permission to go with Pyra if you will agree to watch over her while we're gone."

The two women exchanged glances. If he didn't know better he would think that they were communicating with their minds in the same way that mates could. Eden's hand wandered to her belly like it so frequently did and she seemed to press into a certain area as if she could feel the baby through her skin.

"Are you sure that's what you want?" Eden asked.

Bannack was growing impatient with being questioned. Everyone seemed to think that they knew something he didn't, and it frustrated him. He nodded, not wanting to give her the satisfaction of acknowledging her seeking tone.

"I want to know what's outside this compound. I'm tired of seeing the same things and going the same places. There's more out there and I want to know what it is, but the only way I can do that is to unload Loralia."

"You're the one who brought her here."

"So I've been reminded," Bannack said through gritted teeth.

"If you're sure that's what you want, Bannack, I'll be happy to help her get used to the compound."

"Thank you."

Bannack stepped back out of the bakery and took a deep breath of the night air, hoping it would cool the burning on his cheeks. He didn't know what he wanted anymore, other than to get away.

**TBC**

(To be continued in Part II...)

www.ingramcontent.com/pod-product-compliance
Lightning Source LLC
Chambersburg PA
CBHW032044180726
48284CB00008B/2742